WE'RE EATING MORE BEETS!

Doonesbury books by G. B. Trudeau

Still a Few Bugs in the System
The President Is a Lot Smarter Than You Think
But This War Had Such Promise
Call Me When You Find America
Guilty, Guilty, Guilty!
"What Do We Have for the Witnesses, Johnnie?"
Dare to Be Great, Ms. Caucus
Wouldn't a Gremlin Have Been More Sensible?
"Speaking of Inalienable Rights, Amy . . ."
You're Never Too Old for Nuts and Berries
An Especially Tricky People
As the Kid Goes for Broke
Stalking the Perfect Tan
"Any Grooming Hints for Your Fans, Rollie?"
But the Pension Fund Was Just Sitting There
We're Not Out of the Woods Yet
A Tad Overweight, but Violet Eyes to Die For
And That's My Final Offer!
He's Never Heard of You, Either
In Search of Reagan's Brain
Ask for May, Settle for June
Unfortunately, She Was Also Wired for Sound
The Wreck of the "Rusty Nail"
You Give Great Meeting, Sid
Doonesbury: A Musical Comedy
Check Your Egos at the Door
That's *Doctor* Sinatra, You Little Bimbo!
Death of a Party Animal
Downtown Doonesbury
Calling Dr. Whoopee
Talkin' About My G-G-Generation
We're Eating More Beets!

In Large Format

The Doonesbury Chronicles
Doonesbury's Greatest Hits
The People's Doonesbury
Doonesbury Dossier: The Reagan Years
Doonesbury Deluxe: Selected Glances Askance

A DOONESBURY BOOK BY
G.B. Trudeau

WE'RE EATING MORE BEETS!

AN OWL BOOK · HENRY HOLT AND COMPANY · NEW YORK

USA TODAY: A STATE OF MIND IN SEARCH OF A HEARTBEAT!

WEDNESDAY

Also . . .

WHERE?: ▪ IDAHO. ▪ GEORGIA. ▪ ILLINOIS. ▪ 47 OTHER STATES. **HOW?:** ▪ BY BUS. **WHO?:** ▪ **USA TODAY** FOUNDER AL NEUHARTH. ▪ STAFF. **WHY?:** ▪ TO TAKE PULSE.

Miami
91/77

Boston •
74/58

Concord
76/54

FOCUSING ON FUTURE BUSCAPADES:

NEUHARTH'S DISPATCHES REVEAL A COMMON TOUCH AND LOVE OF COUNTRY NOT SEEN SINCE ANOTHER FAMOUS FOUNDER, **GEORGE WASHINGTON!**

▪ Miami

▪ A high-ranking academic

One-third couldn't smell

▪ A yodeling dog

OTHER SIMILARITIES: ▪ BOTH MEN HAD A VISION ▪ BOTH HAVE BUSTS OF THEMSELVES IN THE WASHINGTON AREA.

Location: Lobby of USA Today Bldg. (How to get there, 1-D.)

Location: Library of Congress

DON'T COUNT THEM OUT

OPINIONLINE

USA TODAY: WHERE DIVERSE OPINIONS CANCEL EACH OTHER OUT!

VOICES

The Debate / Is USA Today

BARBARA BOOPSTEIN
Actress/Channeler
Los Angeles, Calif.

Yes. It costs 50¢, which is what a lot of newspapers go for these days.

MARK SLACKMEYER
Radio Personality
Washington, D.C.

Is the **Pope** Catholic? Isn't **Angie Dickinson** a star? Don't you love everything **Sinatra's** ever recorded? Is **Larry King** a columnist?

ACROSS THE USA:

a newspaper?

ZONKER HARRIS
Socialite
New York, New York

Of course not. But I think they're still protected by the First Amendment.

DAISY DOONESBURY
Farmer
Tulsa, Okla.

I'm not sure. That bus came through and left one of those blue boxes, but Henry ran over it with the tractor.

CONCLUSION? ▪ A RECORD 84% OF US HAVE OPINIONS, ▪ 69% KNOW SOMEONE WHO'S HAD ONE IN THE LAST YEAR!

GB Trudeau

An opposing view

THE LONG AND SHORT OF IT

USA TODAY'S DATELINE

SPEAKS ITS MIND

WE ALWAYS KNEW YOU WOULDN'T AMOUNT TO ANYTHING, SKIPPER!
ME? HEY, I'VE GOT NEWS FOR YA, GEORGIE-PIE...
YOU'VE BEEN STANDING IN REAGAN'S SHADOW FOR SO LONG, YOU'VE COMPLETELY ATROPHIED!
WHAT ARE YOU TALKING ABOUT?
GO AHEAD, TAKE A LOOK! TAKE A HARD LOOK AT YOURSELF!
OH... MY GOD! WHERE'S THE REST OF ME?
SEE? YOU'RE EVEN USING HIS LINES!
GBTrudeau

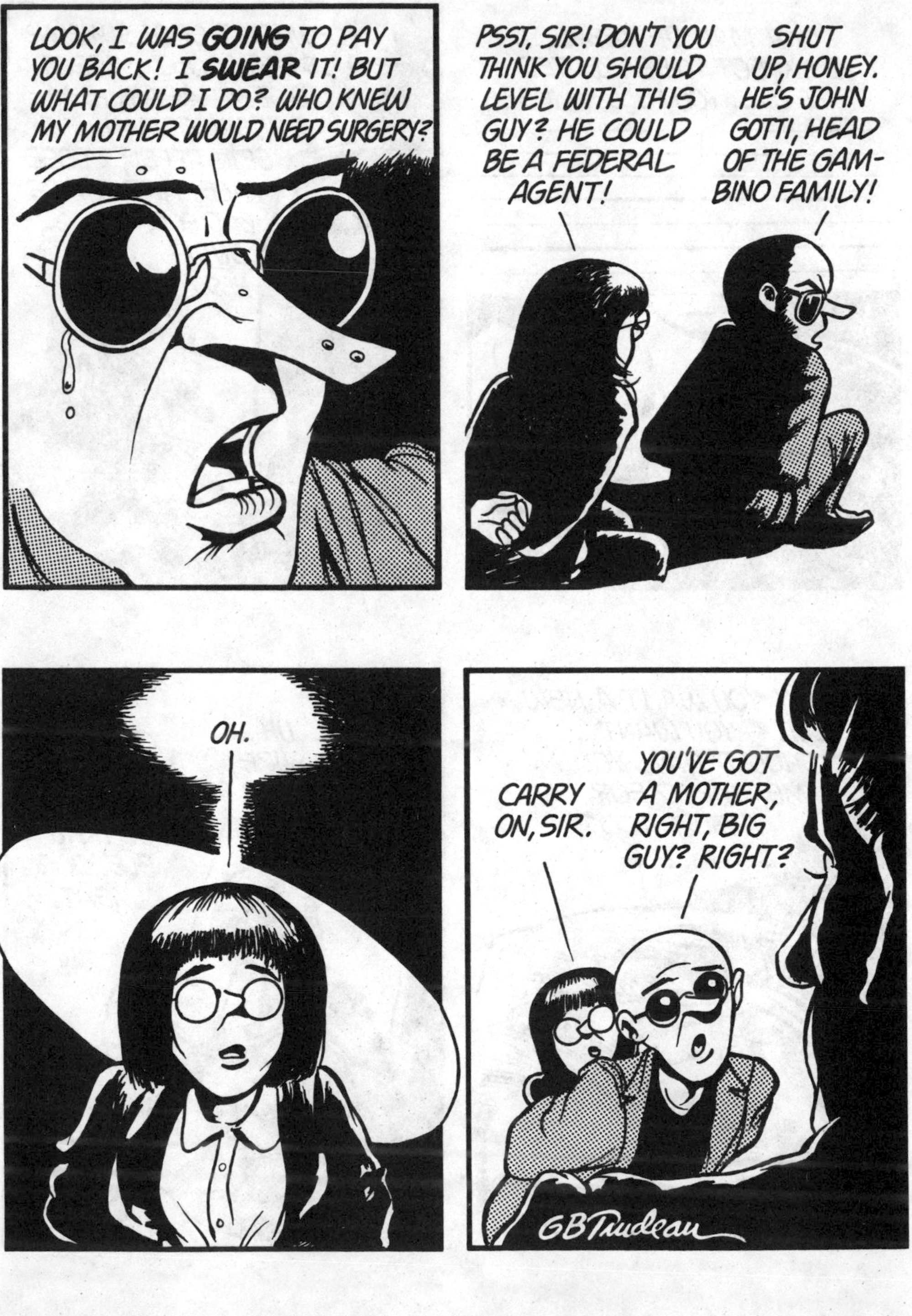
LOOK, I WAS GOING TO PAY YOU BACK! I SWEAR IT! BUT WHAT COULD I DO? WHO KNEW MY MOTHER WOULD NEED SURGERY?
PSST, SIR! DON'T YOU THINK YOU SHOULD LEVEL WITH THIS GUY? HE COULD BE A FEDERAL AGENT!
SHUT UP, HONEY. HE'S JOHN GOTTI, HEAD OF THE GAMBINO FAMILY!
OH.
CARRY ON, SIR.
YOU'VE GOT A MOTHER, RIGHT, BIG GUY? RIGHT?
GBTrudeau

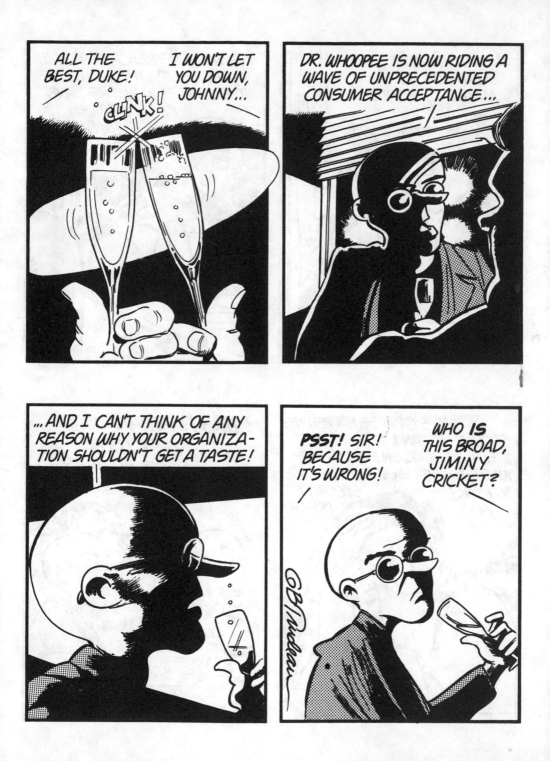

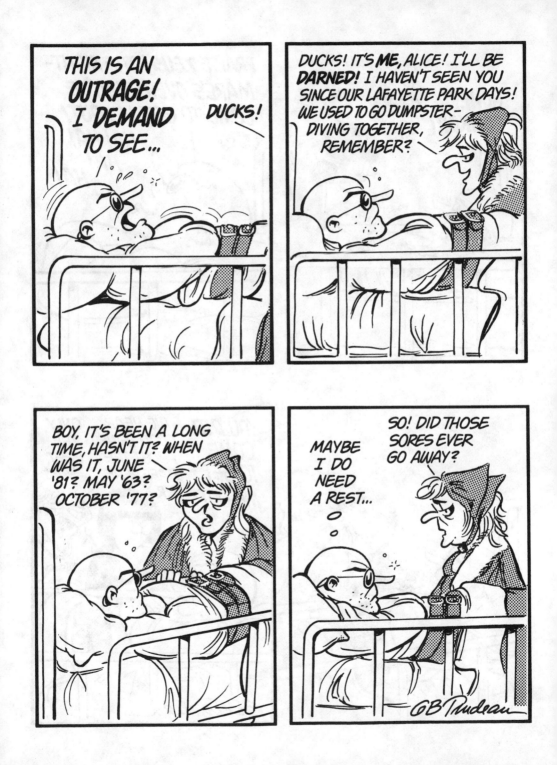

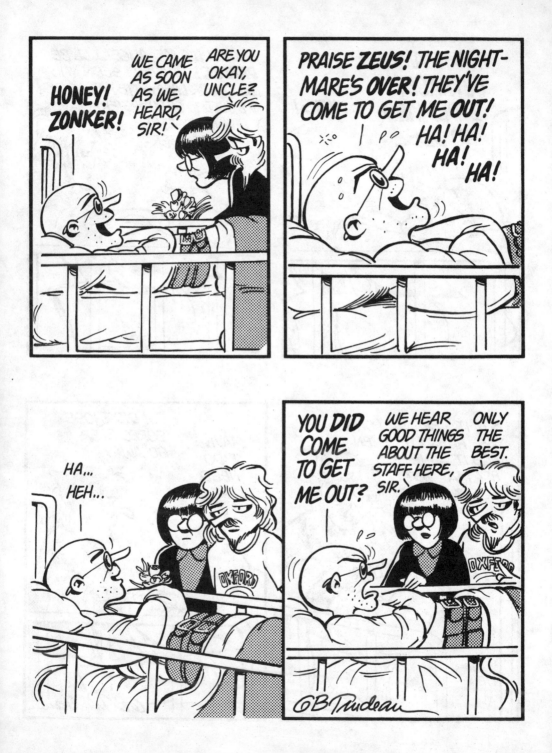

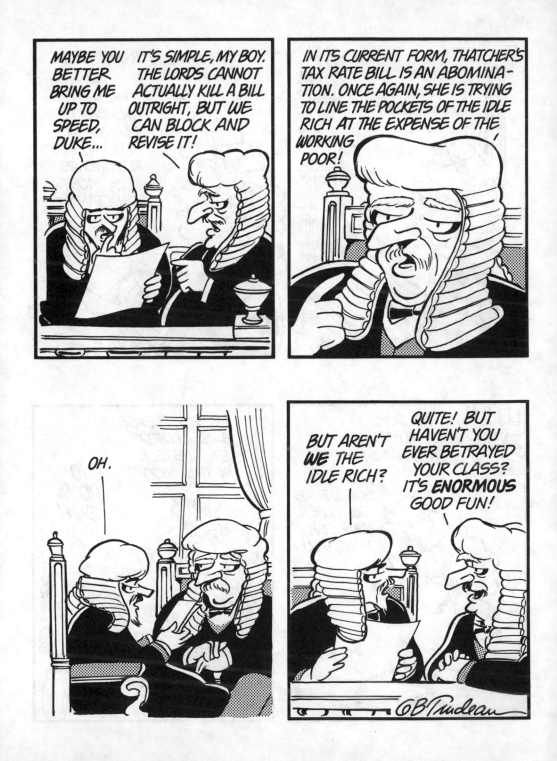

MR. HEADREST, WHAT DO YOU RECALL OF MR. BUSH'S ROLE IN THE IRAN ARMS DEAL?

FRANKLY, NOT THAT MUCH. I'M A NIGHT PERSON, SO I USUALLY SKIP THE CABINET MEETINGS...

BUT I DID MAKE THE JANUARY 7, 1986 MEETING. I RECALL THAT CAP AND GEORGE STRENUOUSLY OBJECTED TO THE WHOLE SCHEME...

...BUT FROM THE BACK OF THE ROOM, A TINY, TINNY VOICE KEPT S-S-SAYING, "I'M UP FOR IT! I'M UP FOR IT!" I TRIED TO SEE WHO IT WAS, BUT HE KEPT CUTTING OUT, OUT!

©B Trudeau

IS THIS THE MAN?

HMM... NO, NO, HE WAS SOFTER AROUND THE EYES.

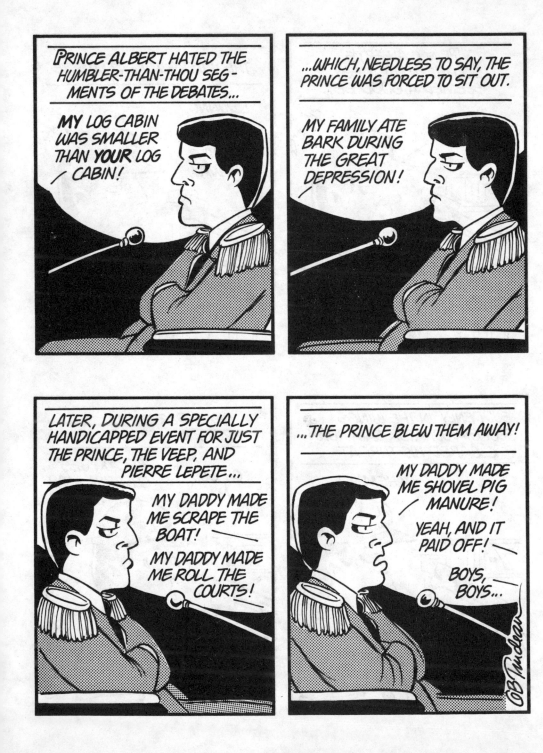

AS THE **OUTSIDER** SPOKE, A BAND OF 30 MORE DESPERADOS QUIETLY SHUFFLED INTO TOWN.

"DON'T BE ALARMED," SAID THE OUTSIDER REASSURINGLY...

THESE PEOPLE **SUPPORT** MY INSURGENCY AGAINST THE ESTABLISH-MENT!

THE TOWNSFOLK WERE HESITANT.

TOUGH-LOOKIN' BUNCH OF HOMBRES...

WHO **ARE** THEY?

MEMBERS OF CONGRESS!

NEXT: WILL THE MEMBERS TAKE THE LAW INTO THEIR OWN HANDS?

GBTrudeau

WELL, HELLO, BENNET!
GOOD EVENING, SIR. I WONDER IF I MIGHT HAVE A WORD WITH YOU.
SURE! WHAT'S UP?
SIR, THE DUKE IS TOO GOOD A HOST TO SAY SO, BUT THE CONSEN-SUS OF THE HOUSEHOLD IS THAT YOU'VE EXHAUSTED HIS HOSPI-TALITY.
I KNOW IT'S NOT MY PLACE TO REPORT THIS, SIR, BUT I THOUGHT YOU SHOULD KNOW.
THANKS, BENNET. SAY, SINCE YOU'RE HERE, I COULD USE SOME MORE BATH SALTS...
I'VE TAKEN THE LIBERTY OF PACKING YOUR BAGS, SIR.
GB Trudeau

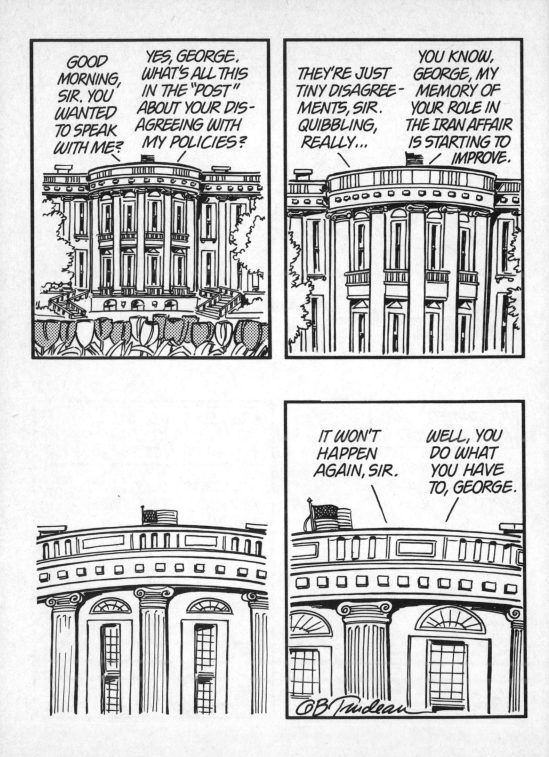